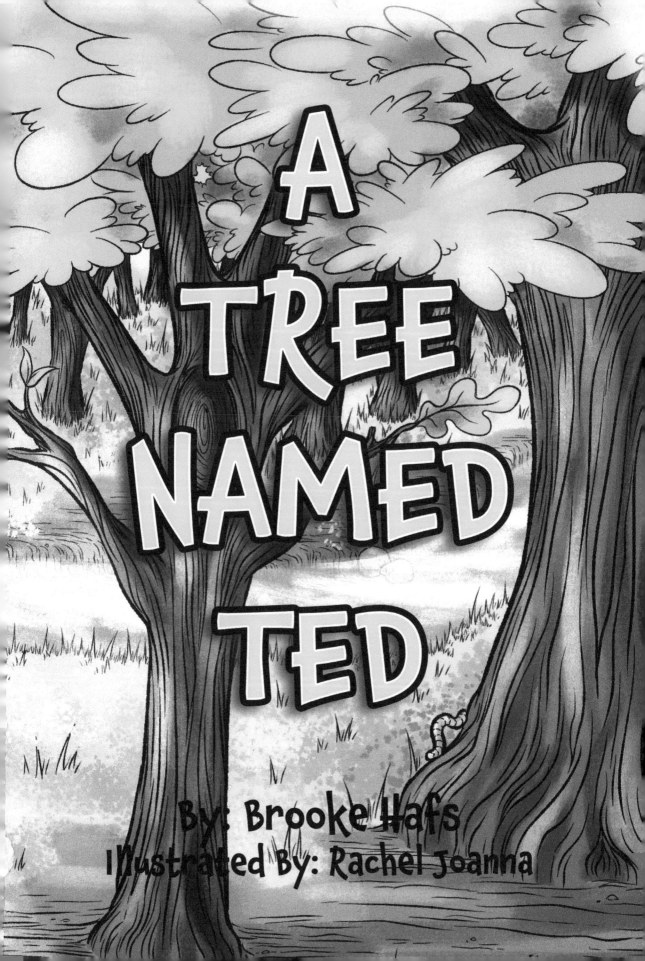

A TREE NAMED TED

By: Brooke Hafs

Illustrated By: Rachel Joanna

A Tree Named Ted
Copyright © 2021 by Brooke Hafs
ISBN 9781645383260

A Tree Named Ted
by Brooke Hafs
Illustrated by Rachel Joanna

For information, please contact:

www.orangehatpublishing.com
Waukesha, WI

To my mom and dad for cultivating my love of nature all throughout my childhood, and for sharing their slice of heaven with me and my kids.

When I was a little girl . . .

I walked in the woods down by the cabin.
I weaved my way through trails
and came to a shady spot by the big oak tree.

The woods were a quiet place where I went to think.
The only sounds were the baby birds chirping
and the babbling brook trickling over the rocks.
I sat on the muddy ground thinking about
things that mattered to me.

A fresh and budding
tree named Ted
spoke to me.
Ted explained that
these years are
for playing and
laughter.

He helped ease my worries and turned them into comfort. Ted was wise, even for a sprout. He told me everything was alright, and I trotted back out of the woods feeling fine.

When I was a teenager . . .

I walked in the woods down by the cabin.
I weaved my way through trails
and came to a secluded spot by the big oak tree.

The woods were a happy place
where I went to think.
The only sounds were the animals
scurrying through the thick brush and
the occasional snap of a twig.
I sat on the dirt floor thinking about
things that mattered to me.

A young and beautiful tree named Ted spoke to me.
Ted explained that these years are
for learning and growing.

He helped ease my concerns
and turned them into cheer.
Ted was wise, even for a sapling.
He told me everything was alright,
and I skipped back out of the
woods feeling fantastic.

When I was a woman . . .

I walked in the woods down by the cabin.
I weaved my way through trails
and came to a scenic spot by the big oak tree.

The woods were a safe place where I went to think. The only sounds were the acorns falling through the trees and the crunch of fallen leaves under my body. I sat on the leaf-covered ground thinking about things that mattered to me.

A sturdy and colorful tree named Ted spoke to me.
Ted explained that these years are for
achieving and appreciating.

He helped ease my fears and
turned them into joy.
Ted was wise, even for a growing tree.
He told me everything was alright,
and I strolled back out of the
woods feeling focused.

When I was old and grey . . .

I walked in the woods down by the cabin.
I weaved my way through trails
and came to a special spot by the big oak tree.

Life

Peace

Happiness

The woods were a familiar place
where I went to think.
The only sounds were the icicles
sliding off tree branches and the crunch
of snow under my weight.
I sat on the cold ground thinking about
things that mattered to me.

A large and thriving tree named Ted spoke to me.
Ted explained that these years are for
reflecting and remembering.

He helped ease my woes
and turned them into peace.
Ted was wise, even for an aging tree.
He told me everything was alright,
and I shuffled back out of the woods
feeling finished.

CPSIA information can be obtained
at www.ICGtesting.com
Printed in the USA
BVHW050753111121
621197BV00006B/691